HELLO, I'M THEA!

I'm *Geronimo Stilton*'s sister. As I'm sure you know from my brother's bestselling novels, I'm a special correspondent for *The Rodent's Gazette*, Mouse Island's most famouse newspaper. Unlike my 'fraidy mouse brother, I absolutely adore traveling, having adventures, and meeting rodents from all around the world!

The adventure I want to tell you about begins at Mouseford Academy, the school I went to when I was a young mouseling. I had such a great experience there as a student that I came back to teach a journalism class.

When I returned as a grown mouse, I met five really special students: Colette, Nicky, Pamela, Paulina, and Violet. You could hardly imagine five more different mouselings, but they became great friends right away. And they liked me so much that they decided to name their group after me: the Thea Sisters! I was so touched by that, I decided to write about their adventures. So turn the page to read a fabumouse adventure about the

THEA SISTERS!

Colette

She has a passion for clothing and style, especially anything pink. When she grows up, she wants to be a fashion editor.

Paulina

Cheerful and kind, she loves traveling and meeting rodents from all over the world. She has a magic touch when it comes to technology.

Violet

She's the bookworm of the group, and she loves learning. She enjoys classical music and dreams of becoming a famouse violinist.

THE THEA SISTERS

Nicky

She comes from Australia and is very enthusiastic about sports and nature. She loves being outside and is always ready to get up and go!

Pamela

She is a great mechanic: Give her a screwdriver and she'll fix anything! She loves pizza, which she eats every day, and she loves to cook.

Do you want to help the Thea Sisters in this new adventure? It's not hard — just follow the clues!

When you see this magnifying glass, pay attention: It means there's an important clue on the page. Each time one appears, we'll review the clues so we don't miss anything.

**ARE YOU READY?
A NEW MYSTERY AWAITS!**

Thea Stilton

AND THE
MOUNTAIN OF
FIRE

Scholastic Inc.

The publisher does not have any control over and does not assume any responsibility for author or third-party websites or their content.

GERONIMO STILTON and THEA STILTON names, characters, and related indicia are copyright, trademark, and exclusive license of Atlantyca S.p.A. All rights reserved. The moral right of the author has been asserted. Based on an original idea by Elisabetta Dami.

geronimostilton.com

Published by Scholastic Inc., *Publishers since 1920*, 557 Broadway, New York, NY 10012. SCHOLASTIC and associated logos are trademarks and/or registered trademarks of Scholastic Inc.

Stilton is the name of a famous English cheese. It is a registered trademark of the Stilton Cheese Makers' Association. For more information, go to www.stiltoncheese.com.

ISBN 978-0-545-15060-6

Text by Thea Stilton
Original title *La montagna parlante*
Cover by Manuela Razzi and Ketty Formaggio
Illustrations by Massimo Asaro, Lucia Balletti, Alessandro Battan, Fabio Bono, Jacopo Brandi, Sergio Cabella, Barbara Di Muzio, Giorgio Di Vita, Marco Failla, Paolo Ferrante, Claudia Forcelloni, Danilo Loizedda, Giada Perissinotto, Manuela Razzi, Federica Salfo, and Luca Usai
Graphics by Merenguita Gingermouse and Michela Battaglin

Special thanks to Beth Dunfey
Translated by Lidia Morson Tramontozzi
Interior design by Kay Petronio

35 34 33 32 31 30   19 20 21 22 23

Printed in the U.S.A.   40
This edition first printing 2019

BOOKS TO READ AND BOOKS TO WRITE

It was a rainy evening in New Mouse City — a perfect night to stay at home and curl up with a good book and a nice cup of **H☺T CHEDDAR**.

"Hmm, what should I read?" I wondered.

Eat, Squeak, Love. I'd read it already.

THE MONA MOUSA CODE. That was a great mystery — one of my brother Geronimo's

Thea Stilton

> Help the members of the Thea Sisters solve the mystery! When you see this magnifying glass, pay attention: It means there's an important clue on that page.

best works — but I'd already read it, too.

Suddenly, the doorbell rang.

RING-RING! RING-RING! RING-RING!

A high, *screechy* voice shouted from the other side of the door, "Hey, is anybody home? **Helloooo!?**"

I'd recognize that squeak anywhere. It belonged to the grumpy but lovable **Mercury whale**, the mailmouse for **MOUSEFORD ACADEMY**. Mouseford Academy is a famouse school on Whale Island. I studied there as a mouseling and had recently returned as a visiting professor.

"Mercury!" I exclaimed, throwing open the door.

"Hello, Professor Stilton," Mercury said. "Nice to see you. I have a package for

Mercury Whale

you." He thrust a yellow package with a pink bow into my paws. The label read:

To our dearest friend and teacher
Thea Stilton

It was followed by five familiar signatures: Colette, Nicky, Pamela, PAULINA, and **Violet**.

What a lovely surprise! It was a package from my favorite students, five mouselings I had gotten to know at Mouseford when I returned to teach there. In addition to passing my investigative journalism course with flying colors, the five mice had helped me solve a mystery. I'd become a mentor to the mouselings, and they'd decided to name themselves after me: the Thea Sisters.

I said good-bye to Mercury. I couldn't

wait to see what the Thea Sisters had sent! I ripped open the package. Inside was a beautiful wool **sweater** and a long, **loooooooooong** letter.

I put on the sweater. Fabumouse! It fit me perfectly. And it was so soft!

I sat down on the sofa and began reading the *letter*. By the time I reached the middle of the second page, I knew exactly how I would spend the rest of the evening. I had found a new book to write! It would be a book about the latest incredible adventure of the Thea Sisters!

I'm going to call it **THE MOUNTAIN OF FIRE!**

Pamela

Nicky

Colette

Violet

PAULINA

My Friends, the Thea Sisters

AUSTRALIA

A PHONE CALL FROM AUSTRALIA

The Thea Sisters' adventure began simply—with a phone call. It was for *Nicky* and it came all the way from her home in Australia.

The call was from Nicky's grandmother Naya. **NAYA** was an Australian Aborigine.

"Nicky, I'm so sorry to **BOTHER** you," Naya said. "But your parents are traveling, and I can't get in touch with them."

Nicky's whiskers **quivered** with worry. She'd never heard her **beloved** grandmother sound so stressed.

"What's wrong, Naya?" Nicky asked.

Naya

"Strange things are happening at the ranch," Naya said. "The SHEEP in the middle pen are sick."

"Have you called the vet?" Nicky asked.

"Yes, but he can't figure out what's wrong," Naya replied. "I just don't know what to do."

"I'm coming home to help you, Naya!" Nicky vowed. "I'll be there as soon as I can."

Nicky hung up the phone and immediately started packing.

THE AUSTRALIAN ABORIGINES

The Aborigines are the native people of Australia. They have lived in Australia for at least 50,000 years and possibly as long as 65,000 years!

The term *Aborigine* is used to describe any indigenous Australian, but, in fact, there are as many as 500 different clans, each with its own territory and language. Yet all the clans share a deep spiritual connection to the land. Today, Aborigines make up more than 2 percent of the total population of Australia.

"WHAT'S GOING ON, NICK?" PAULINA asked. Paulina was Nicky's roommate and closest friend at Mouseford Academy.

"There's an emergency at home," Nicky explained. "I need to go back to Australia as soon as possible. My parents are away, and our SHEEP are sick. My grandmother needs my help."

Colette put her paw on Nicky's shoulder. (By this time, she, Violet, and Pamela had gathered around their friend.) "You are such a kindhearted mouse! I'm sure your sheep will be OK."

Nicky smiled. "Thanks for trying to **cheer me up**, Colette. But the sheep are not our pets; they are our BUSINESS. We shear their WOOL and sell it. We

depend on them to keep the ranch going."

"But, Nicky, we're right in the middle of the school term," Violet said. "Can you really just pick up and leave right now?"

"I don't have a choice," Nicky said. "My grandmother needs me. I've got to go!"

Paulina, Violet, Pamela, and Colette exchanged looks. They could tell Nicky had made up her mind.

"We're coming, too!" Pamela said.

"That's right!" agreed **Violet.**

"You're not going all by yourself!"

Nicky was full of *gratitude*. She *threw her paws* around her friends. "Thanks so much! You're the **best friends** a mouseling could ever want!"

"Well, come on then," said Violet. She wasn't a mushy type of mouse. "Let's go talk to **Professor de Mousus**."

WE'RE LEAVING!

Octavius de Mousus, the headmaster of **MOUSEFORD** is the kind of rodent who seems really stern, but underneath that stiff fur beats a heart of gold.

Professor de Mousus listened carefully to the **Thea Sisters**. "My dear mouselings, you know no student is allowed to leave the academy during the semester," he squeaked kindly. "But, since this is an emergency, I will grant you permission to leave Whale Island. **HOWEVER**, when you return, you will still need to take your exams. So don't neglect your *studies*!"

Octavius de Mousus

The mouselings nodded. "Thank you, Professor!" said Nicky. "We won't forget."

Early the following morning, the five mouselings headed down to the port to catch a boat back to New Mouse City. Quite a few rodents came to see them off.

As the ship began moving slowly away from the dock, Mercury whale and his brothers broke into a farewell tune.

THE HYMN FOR A HAPPY RETURN

May your journey be a breeze,

Rich with smiles and rich with cheese!

May your return be filled with delight.

We'll await your arrival day and night

When you return, we'll all eat cheesecake.

But don't forget to bring us a keepsake!

ARE WE THERE YET?

In New Mouse city, the five friends caught a plane to Australia, which was practically on the other side of the world!

Pamela was very excited. She kept asking her friends, **"Are we there yet? How much longer?"**

The next thing the mouselings knew,

Are we there yet?

How much longer?

Pam had asked the pilot and all the other passengers, **"Are we there yet? How much longer?"**

Colette leaned over to Paulina. "If Pam had to parachute down, she'd probably ask a passing seagull, **'Are we there yet? Will it take much longer?'"**

Paulina and Colette giggled behind their paws.

ONLY 250 MILES TO GO!

The Thea Sisters's plane landed in Sydney, the largest city in Australia.

"Holey cheese, that was a long trip!" Paulina said, rubbing her sore tail.

Nicky smiled at her friends. "Sisters, I have good news and bad news. The bad news is that our trip's not over yet."

Billy, Nicky's cousin

Her friends squeaked in protest.

"So what's the good news?" Colette asked.

"My cousin **Billy** is here waiting for us!" Nicky exclaimed. She waved her hat at a good-looking rodent who was leaning against a **pink**, **flowered** camper.

Nicky gave her cousin a big hug. "Billy's going to take us to the ranch," she told her friends.

"G'day, everyone!" said Billy. "Climb in!"

The Thea Sisters and Billy piled into the camper. After an hour on the road, it was Violet and Paulina who were asking, "**Are we there yet? How much longer?**"

Billy just smiled. "Easy on, mouselings! Only another 250 miles to go."

Colette's fur turned white. "What do you mean, only another 250 miles?"

Billy pointed to the horizon. "Australia is an enormouse continent, **SO EVERYTHING IS RELATIVE!**"

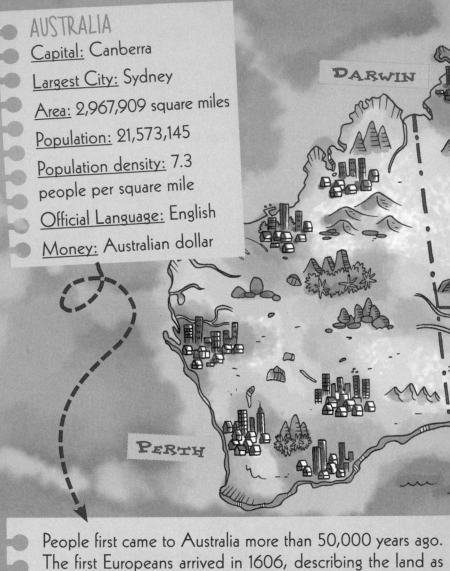

AUSTRALIA

<u>Capital</u>: Canberra

<u>Largest City</u>: Sydney

<u>Area</u>: 2,967,909 square miles

<u>Population</u>: 21,573,145

<u>Population density</u>: 7.3 people per square mile

<u>Official Language</u>: English

<u>Money</u>: Australian dollar

DARWIN

PERTH

People first came to Australia more than 50,000 years ago. The first Europeans arrived in 1606, describing the land as *Terra Australis, Incognita*, which means "unknown southern land." Then, in 1770, the famous British explorer Captain James Cook mapped the eastern coast and claimed the land in the name of the king of England. The British established six colonies on the continent from 1788 to 1868.

Flinders Ranges National Park

Nicky's Family's Ranch

In 1901, the six British colonies joined together to form an independent federation called the Commonwealth of Australia. The king or queen of England is the official head of state and is represented by the governor-general in Australia.

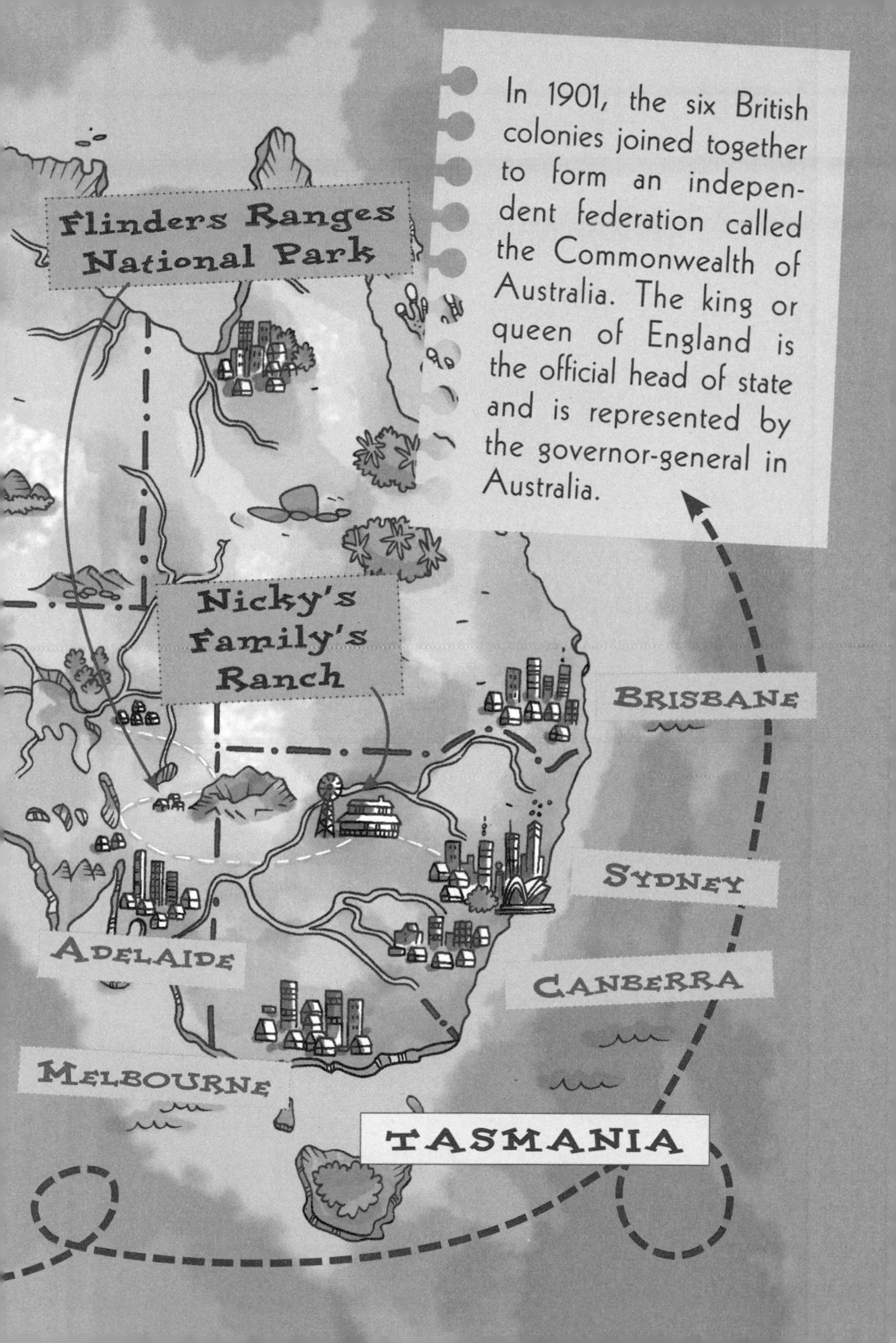

BRISBANE

SYDNEY

ADELAIDE

CANBERRA

MELBOURNE

TASMANIA

FINALLY HOME!

Billy and the Thea Sisters traveled the entire night. The camper drove over **MOUNTAINS** and **VALLEYS**. The road had so many twists and turns that Violet turned a little green. "I can't take it anymore! I think I'm going to **LOSE MY CHEESE**!"

Nicky laughed. "Just hold on, Vi! This ride's about to get a lot less BUMPY."

Nicky was right. A moment later, the camper came to a **wide-open** prairie. The **moon** was high in the sky. It glinted off the grass, which was sparkling with new dew. "What a GORGEOUS place!" exclaimed Paulina. "It looks like a fairyland."

The mouselings could see spots that looked like **snowy bushes**. As the camper drew nearer, they realized that the spots were, in fact, huge herds of SHEEP.

Nicky and Billy took turns DRIVING. Violet, Paulina, Pamela, and Colette took turns ratnapping and keeping the drivers company.

As the van sped across the prairie, Nicky's thoughts turned to the reason they were

there. "I'm almost afraid to ask, Billy, but is there any news from the ranch?"

Billy's cheerful expression DARKENED. "Let's not worry about that now. We'll be there soon."

In the wee hours of the morning, Nicky let out a shout. "**There it is!**" She pointed to a big, ramshackle farmhouse in the distance. She smiled a little sadly. "It's always good to be home, no matter what the reason."

A few moments later, the mouselings reached the ranch.

Bong! Bong! Bong!

Nicky's grandmother, Naya, was standing at the farmhouse door. She was beating a pot with a metal ladle. "**LET'S GO, MOUSELINGS!** Move your tails! I've made you a delicious breakfast of eggs and cheese grits. You don't want to eat them cold, **DO YOU**?"

"Naya!" Nicky cried. "It's so **good** to see you!"

AUSTRALIAN STATIONS

Everything in Australia is huge, even the ranches, which are known as stations. The interior of the continent, the Outback, an area of deserts, red-baked earth, and ancient mountains, is home to these vast cattle and sheep stations.

These ranches are often so isolated that their residents use airplanes to visit their next-door neighbors! Mail and supplies arrive by air, too. Children who live in the Outback don't go to regular school. They either go to boarding school, like Nicky, or they attend the School of the Air. In the past, the teaching medium was a pedal-powered radio. Today, teachers give lessons via satellite dishes and computers. Students can watch and respond via a webcam attached to their computers.

NICKY'S FAMILY'S RANCH

1. The middle pen, where the herd is gathered for shearing.

2. Nicky's house.

3. The stable where the horses sleep. Nicky's favorite horse, Stella, has her own special stall.

4. The garage.

5. The Old Snail (the oldest tractor on the ranch).

6. The silos, where food for the livestock is kept.

7. The horse pen.

8. The windmill, which generates power for the ranch.

9. The pasture, where the herd eats.

"Come here and give me a hug, MY LiTTLE CHEESE DUMPLiNG!" Naya cried, throwing her paws around Nicky.

"Are you OK?" Nicky asked, trying to hold back tears.

"Of course, I am," said Naya, hugging her **tighter**. "Now enough of this! Scamper off and eat with your friends. We'll have plenty of time to talk about our troubles later."

With that, Billy, Nicky, and the rest of the **Thea Sisters** threw themselves on the big, hearty breakfast Naya had made for them. They were famished, and the food was whisker-licking good!

A STRANGE
SICKNESS

When everyone had eaten, Naya led Nicky and PAULINA to the middle pen. All the sick SHEEP were there. They were eating, but they looked tired. Wool was falling from their backs, dotting the Prairie with white tufts.

"Moldy mozzarella!" cried Nicky. "The Great Shearing will take place in less than a month, and we won't have any wool to sell!"

"What's The Great Shearing?" PAULINA asked. She pulled on a pair of plastic gloves and carefully picked up samples of soil and grass to analyze.

WOOL

"These are WOOL sheep," explained Nicky, reaching down to hug one. "Every year, at the end of the cold season, we shear them — that is, we cut off their wool. Once all the sheep are sheared, we sell the wool to factories that use it to make yarn for sweaters, and cloth for dresses and blankets."

"Poor things!" PAULINA exclaimed. "Does the shearing hurt them?"

"Oh, no, of course not!" Nicky replied. "As long as it's done well, and *gently*. It's kind of like getting a furcut."

Paulina wanted to pet the sheep, but the closer she got, the more **nervous** the sheep became. They stomped their hooves and **pressed** against one another.

Nicky's sheep are usually relaxed and calm, but now they seem nervous and anxious. What's wrong?

Paulina tried to **REASSURE** them. "It's okay, little ones! I just want to see if you're alright." She turned to Nicky. "Are they acting like this because they don't know me?"

Nicky shook her snout. "No, there's something **wrong**. They're usually very friendly. If they get frightened, they just run away. I've been around SHEEP my whole life, and I've never seen one stomp its hoofs before."

Nicky was worried. The sheep were obviously sick, and The Great Shearing was coming up soon. There was no way her

baa! baa!

Clue!

parents would be back in time. It was up to her to **take care** of things.

Nicky shivered. She was just a mouseling. How could she take on **so much** responsibility? But on the other paw, how could she not? If she did nothing, the SHEEP would just get sicker. They might even die.

She had to do something! But what?

MERINO SHEEP

Merino sheep are the most valued in the world for the fine quality of their wool. They were first brought to Australia in 1797. Since then, there have been more sheep than people in Australia. Today there are 120 million sheep in Australia — and only 21 million Australians. About 90 million of the sheep are merinos. Wool is one of Australia's main exports. Goulburn, Australia, is home to an enormous concrete-and-steel statue of a merino ram, nicknamed the Big Merino. The statue, which is almost 50 feet tall and weighs nearly 107 tons, is a popular tourist attraction.

A MYSTERIOUS AIRPLANE

"What do I do?" wailed Nicky.

Paulina put her paws around her friend. "**Don't worry!** We're here to help. Let's think. What would **Thea** do?"

Nicky wiped her eyes. "Thanks, Paulina. You're right. Let's not lose our snouts." She took a deep breath. "OK, if Thea were here, she'd review the situation, make a **LIST**, and figure out her next move."

Here's what the list looked like:

- Something must be making the sheep sick.
- Only the sheep in the middle pen are sick. So the sickness isn't contagious.
- All the sheep on the ranch drink from the same stream. Therefore, the water is not the cause of the sickness.

CONCLUSION: If something is making the sheep sick, it has to be in the grass of the middle pen.

Paulina went inside to take a closer look at her **soil samples**. Pam, Colette, and Violet went along to help her.

Nicky and Billy worked with the ranch hands to move all the sheep to another pasture. Once they were done, Nicky decided to visit her favorite horse, Stella. The HAPPY neighing that greeted her quickly made her forget all her worries.

I missed you so much!

"Stella!" she whispered. "*I missed you so much!*" She offered the horse an apple as a snack. Then she threw a saddle over Stella's back and jumped on. Together they **GALLOPED** out onto the open prairie.

Nicky sighed with

happiness. Studying at **MOUSEFORD** was wonderful, and Whale Island was a fantastic place, but there really was no place like home. It felt so good to be back *on the ranch* with the wind rushing through her fur.

Suddenly, Stella neighed loudly and bucked. Fortunately, Nicky was an experienced rider, and she managed to keep her seat. (A less experienced rider would have been thrown from the saddle for sure!)

"What is it?" Nicky asked her horse. *"What's wrong?"*

Stella whinnied and pointed her nose toward the sky. A small plane was circling overhead. This was nothing **UNUSUAL** — all the ranches owned small planes. They were used to visit friends, FERTILIZE the fields, and travel long distances. Yet Stella seemed bothered by it.

Nicky frowned. She realized she'd been gone longer than she thought. It was time to return to the ranch.

She had just led Stella back to the stables when Paulina scurried toward her. "There's **LEAD** in the soil! All the tests are clear. And Violet went **ONLINE** to do a little research, and the sheep's symptoms agree with my diagnosis. Tiredness, loss of fur, and irritability are all signs of **LEAD** poisoning!"

Nicky was stunned. "But how did lead get into the pen?"

Paulina frowned. "I don't know. Maybe the field was watered with **contaminated** water."

NAYA came and joined them. "The plane!" she said. "One night, I heard a plane flying very low over our **RANCH**."

"At night?" asked Nicky in surprise. "That's dangerous!"

"Yes, it's very dangerous," Naya agreed. "But **darkness** is the best cover for rodents who wish to stay **hidden**!" Her snout was creased with worry. "I didn't realize the connection until just now. Soon after I heard that plane, our sheep began losing their **WOOL**!"

"There are only two planes around here." Nicky's whiskers began quivering with anger. "One is ours, and the other belongs to that good-for-nothing sewer rat **Mortimer MacCardigan**!"

THAT GOOD-FOR-NOTHING SEWER RAT!

Quicker than a **kangaroo**, *Nicky* jumped on Stella's back and **GALLOPED** away. She was headed toward **Mortimer MacCardigan**'s ranch. He was their neighbor, and he also raised 𝔖𝔥𝔢𝔢𝔭. In fact, he'd tried to buy their land time and time again. Nicky's parents had always refused, but Mortimer just wouldn't give up. He'd even threatened them once or twice.

Mortimer MacCardigan

Mortimer MacCardigan is Nicky and Naya's neighbor. Like Nicky and her family, he breeds sheep. But Mortimer is ruthless about being the best. He is a self-made rat with no consideration for other rodents.

If Nicky's sheep were **sick**, her family would sell less wool. That might mean they'd have to **SELL** their ranch. And Nicky knew Mortimer MacCardigan would be ready and waiting to buy it from them! Nicky wasn't about to let that happen.

Nicky and Stella finally reached the MacCardigans' ranch. Mortimer was on the **PORCH** with his son, **Nate**. When Mortimer saw Nicky, he started to choke. "Miss Nicky! cough, cough, cough! What a surprise! cough, cough, cough! I thought you were off at that beautiful academy up on Whale Island. cough, cough, cough!"

As he squeaked, he pushed a yellow plastic container under the table. Nicky was so angry she didn't notice.

Nate MACCARDIGAN

36

"Mr. MacCardigan!" she shouted. "There's **LEAD** in my grazing pastures!"

Mortimer MacCardigan turned **RED** from the tip of his snout to the tip of his tail. He looked like a rodent who's been cornered by a hungry cat!

Uh-oh! Nicky didn't notice, but Mortimer MacCardigan hid something under the table!

Clue:

"What are you saying, Miss Nicky?" he stammered. "Are you accusing me of something? How dare you! If you don't get your tail off my property, I'll have you arrested for **TRESPASSING!**"

Nicky clenched her paws. She just knew Mortimer MacCardigan was responsible for her sheep's illness! But she didn't have any real proof. So she CLIMBED back on Stella and headed back to her ranch.

Nate tried to wave good-bye, but Nicky was too upset to notice. "**Hah! Hah!** I got pretty lucky there, didn't I?" said Mortimer.

Nate looked at his father, puzzled.

"That busymouse almost caught me!" Mortimer continued. He pulled out the yellow plastic container. On the side was a **label** with two big letters: **Pb**. It was the chemical symbol for lead!

Nate was **shocked**. He was a very mild-mannered mouse who usually obeyed his father, but he had to **squeak** up at this.

"Dad, how could you?" he asked. **"THAT'S NOT RIGHT!** That's no way to treat sheep, and it's certainly no way to treat our neighbors. It's just not right!"

Mortimer MacCardigan turned **REDDER** than a fire engine. "Don't talk to your father that way!" he growled. "I'll decide what's right or **WRONG**, not you. You watch your tongue, or I'll have your fur!"

THE LAND OF OUR ANCESTORS

When Nicky returned to the ranch, Naya was busy preparing dinner. Nicky joined Billy and the Thea Sisters around the FIRE. A few moments later, Naya sat down next to her.

As they munched on Naya's delicious cheese stew, Nicky told them what had happened with **Mortimer MacCardigan**. "After squeaking with that greedy **sewer rat**, I'm even more convinced he's behind what happened to our SHEEP!" she said. "I think he has a GUILTY conscience."

Nicky turned to Paulina. "Did you find a cure in your research?"

Her friend shook her snout SADLY. "Nothing!"

"I think I might have an idea," said Naya. Nicky **BRIGHTENED** instantly. "Really, Naya? What is it?"

"Perhaps it's time to turn to the wisdom of our ELDERS." She got a faraway look on her snout. "You see, thousands and thousands of years ago, our ancestors used flowers, leaves, and roots to heal all living things. When I was just a tiny mouseling, my grandmother's grandfather told me of a powerful root that could cure every disease."

As she was talking, Naya slipped a necklace of **seeds** from her neck. In the center was a medallion engraved with a **desert mouse**. She gave it to Nicky. "This medallion is the symbol of our *clan*. Take the necklace. It will be of help to you in the land of our ancestors."

Nicky didn't understand. "What do you mean, **NAYA**?"

ANIMAL TOTEMS

A **totem** is a symbol of the special relationship between a person and an animal, place, or object. Each Aborigine has a totem that represents his or her spiritual identity. This identity is usually revealed around the time of birth.

Aboriginal clans also have their own totems that connect the spirits of a clan's people with their ancestors, important places, and other living beings. The totem of Naya's clan is the desert mouse. In their language, its name is *mingkiri*.

Naya pointed northwest.

"Take the necklace with you on your journey. You must go to the **FLINDERS RANGES** and look for Nepabunna. There you will find our clan's ELDERS. They'll know how to help save our sheep."

Naya got up and pulled a smooth, flat, oval piece of wood from a pouch at her waist. A long string was connected to it. Naya grabbed the end of the rope and began *spinning* it over her head.

FAST! FASTER! FASTER!

The wood twisted and turned in the air. It began to make a strange buzzing sound.

Wooo! Wooo! Wooo! Wooo!

The sound kept getting louder and stronger.

Wooo! Wooo! Wooo! Wooo!

It seemed to fill the sky for miles and miles around them.

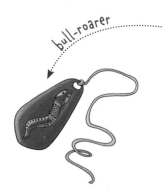

bull-roarer

Violet, PAULINA, *Pamela*, and *Colette* were mesmerized.

"What is it?" Violet asked **Billy**.

"It's called a bull-roarer," he answered. "We use it as a kind of telephone. Whoever hears the sound spins his or her bull-roarer and sends the message, too, until the message finally reaches its destination."

Naya stopped spinning her instrument. "Everything's **FINE**," she said. "Thanks to the bull-roarer, **news of your trip is already on its way to Nepabunna!**"

ABORIGINAL TOOLS AND INSTRUMENTS

The **boomerang** is a piece of curved wood used for hunting. If a hunter misses his or her target, the boomerang returns to him.

The **bull-roarer** is a piece of flat wood tied to a long rope. If it's spun around very fast, it makes a sound so loud that it can be heard many miles away. The speed at which it is spun modifies the sound, making it possible to send different messages.

The **didgeridoo** is a musical instrument made from a branch of eucalyptus or bamboo whose interior had been hollowed out by termites. It can communicate over large distances, much like the bull-roarer. The didgeridoo is probably the oldest musical instrument in the world. Traditionally, only men play this instrument.

Clapsticks are wooden sticks that are banged against each other. They are often decorated with a clan's designs.

Flying Doctors

TED, THE FLYING DOCTOR!

Nicky, Violet, and Pamela spent the rest of the night studying MAPS. Paulina did research on the Internet. Colette calculated the distance from the farm to the **FLINDERS RANGES**.

Before curling up for a good night's sleep, the mouselings started packing for the trip.

"Be sure to bring only what's **absolutely necessary**!" Nicky warned them. She looked at Colette. "Just one *small suitcase* each."

"Why are you looking at me?" Colette cried. "I'll be good, I **promise**!"

The next morning, the five friends were asleep when a droning noise woke them.

FLINDERS RANGES
NATIONAL PARK

The Flinders Ranges is Australia's largest mountain range. Located in southern Australia, it is part of a large national park that is rich in flora and fauna.

FLINDERS RANGES

ADELAIDE

MELBOURNE

Emus, kangaroos, and yellow-footed rock wallabies make their homes here.

The park includes a huge natural amphitheater, Wilpena Pound, surrounded by reddish cliffs that are more than 3,000 feet tall. This area is also home to the Yourambulla caves, whose walls preserve ancient Aboriginal paintings and rock engravings, as well as Sacred Canyon, a narrow, rocky gorge decorated with many rock engravings of kangaroos, emus, and symbolic circles.

Ted, Billy's brother (and Naya's grandson!)

"What's that sound?" Violet **mumbled sleepily**.

"It's a plane!" shouted Nicky, leaping up. She was afraid it might be Mortimer MacCardigan coming back to poison her sheep.

But when she scampered out to the porch, she saw a **WHITE PLANE** with an odd *crest* painted on the fuselage. It was the logo of the Royal Flying Doctor Service!

The plane landed on the ranch's lawn. Billy ran toward the friendly-looking pilot, a rat wearing a *flashy*, flowered shirt.

Billy introduced him to Nicky's friends. "This is Doctor Oodgeroo Yunupingu of the **Royal Flying Doctor Service**. But you can call him Ted. He's my brother!"

"G'day, everyone!" Ted said. He hugged Nicky. "It's been

THE ROYAL FLYING DOCTOR SERVICE OF AUSTRALIA

What happens if you get a stomachache in the heart of Australia and the nearest doctor is hundreds of miles away? Call the Flying Doctors!

The first Australian Flying Doctor's flight took place on May 15, 1928. From then on, the Flying Doctors have been on duty 24 hours a day, seven days a week. From July 1, 2007, through June 30, 2008, they saw more than 260,000 patients (averaging 717 calls a day), flying from one end of Australia to the other for a total of more than 14.4 million miles a year. That's like flying around the world almost 600 times!

TOO LONG, Cousin."

Billy and Ted helped the **Thea Sisters** load their baggage onto the plane. Pam had her backpack and her wrench (she never left home without it). Paulina had a duffel bag and her laptop. Violet had a shoulder bag and a teeny-weeny **pumpkin house** that held **Frilly**, her pet cricket. Nicky had a small knapsack and a pair of **bin⊙⊕ulars**.

Everyone had taken Nicky's words to **heart** and packed light. Everyone, that is, except Colette. She was carrying a tiny *pink* purse and an **ENORMOUSE** suitcase that looked like it was about to *BURST* open.

Nicky, Paulina, Pamela, and Violet stared at her.

"*What is it?*" Colette asked "What's wrong?

I packed one suitcase, just like you said and it's not even completely **full**!"

Nobody said anything. They just kept staring at her. Finally, Colette sighed and went back into the farmhouse, dragging the enormouse suitcase behind her. A few minutes later, she emerged again. This time, she was carrying only the little purse and a small **BACKPACK**.

"I don't know what I'll do if we get invited to a *dance*," Colette worried as she climbed on the plane. "I'll have nothing to wear!"

Nicky gently placed her paw on her shoulder. "Don't worry, Colette! If somebody asks you to a dance, I'll get you a dress, I promise."

TRAVELING IN AUSTRALIA

If you're traveling in Australia, don't forget any of these essentials:

- a map of the area
- bug spray
- a hat and sunscreen
- lots of water
- light clothes for the days and a sweater for cool nights
- raingear during the rainy season (December through March)
- a radio or cell phone with all the necessary numbers programmed
- basic first aid knowledge

iT WAS SUPPOSED TO BE A RELAXiNG FLiGHT . . .

A few moments later, the plane took off. "The **Flinders Ranges** aren't too far away, and I'll take you there from go to whoa," Doctor Ted told the five friends. "It's a short flight — just three hundred miles. So sit back and get comfy! You're flying the friendly skies."

Nicky smiled. She loved flying. And she felt better now that they had a plan.

It was **SUPPoSED** to be a relaxing flight, but it **WASN'T** at all.

Mortimer MacCardigan had spotted Doctor Ted's plane *TAKING OFF*. Ever since Nicky's visit, Mortimer MacCardigan had worried that Nicky would **FOIL** his plans. So he had started spying on her ranch with a pair of binoculars.

When Mortimer MacCardigan saw Doctor Ted's plane take off, he had a nasty idea. He called the Royal Flying Doctor Service and pretended he had an emergency.

"**Help me! Help me!** I'm a poor, very sick rodent! I reeeeeally need help!"

A *polite* nurse answered his call. "CALM DOWN, sir, and tell me exactly where you live!"

The plane with the Thea Sisters had taken off toward the **WEST**. So Mortimer told the nurse he lived around Buckleboo.

Nepabunna

Buckleboo

Ranch

Port Augusta

Adelaide

Sydney

Melbourne

"You're lucky," said the nurse. "Doctor Ted is flying in that direction right now, toward Nepabunna. I'll tell him to **make a stop** in Buckleboo."

"Thank you!" squeaked Mortimer. "Thank you so much!" He hung up the phone, grinning with satisfaction.

Unfortunately for him, Nate had overheard the whole conversation. "Dad, what are you doing?"

"What has to be done!" Mortimer barked GRUFFLY. "In business, sometimes you have to bend the truth."

Nate shook his snout. "Poisoning sheep isn't bending the truth. It's **SABOTAGE**! And lying to the Royal Flying Doctor Service is just wrong. What if someone were really sick?"

Mortimer MacCardigan turned **PURPLE**, then **red**. "Scamper upstairs and pack your

I want to Know!

backpack! I'll teach you what's right and what's wrong!"

Nate didn't understand. "Where are we going?"

"That's for me to know and you to find out!" exclaimed Mortimer.

"I want to know what that busymouse is up to!"

In the meantime, Doctor Ted had received the order to change his route. "I'm sorry, Nicky! Dispatch just told me there's an **EMERGENCY** in Buckleboo. There's a rodent desperately in need of medical attention, and I can't take you with me. It's against the rules. I'll have to drop you off in Port Augusta."

TiC! TiC! TiC! PLOP! PLOP! PLOP! SPLASH! SPLASH!

Doctor Ted was a rodent of his word. He dropped Nicky and her friends off at the **PORT AUGUSTA** train station. An hour later, they were on board a TRAIN headed north to the city of Hawker. At Hawker, they scurried to the bus for Wilpena. There they went to a car rental shop to rent an SUV.

The mouse who rented them the SUV was cheerful. "This baby's got everything you need for an absolutely fabumouse adventure!" he promised.

FLINDERS RANGES NATIONAL PARK

Nepabunna

Wilpena

Hawker

Port Augusta

Adelaide

They piled into the SUV and set off. The scenery was **BREATHTAKING**! They passed rolling **GREEN VALLEYS** and meadows and giant trees. Pamela, Colette, Violet, and Paulina **BOUNCED** from one side of the SUV to the other, peering out the windows. Soon they started a contest to see who could spot the most animals. *A parrot! An eagle!*

"What's that cute little critter? Is it a **BABY KANGAROO**?"

"That's not a kangaroo, that's a wallaby," Nicky explained.

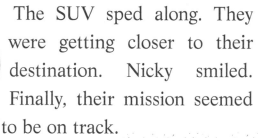

The SUV sped along. They were getting closer to their destination. Nicky smiled. Finally, their mission seemed to be on track.

But just then, a soft, light rain began to fall.

Tic! Tic! Tic! Tic! Tic! Tic! Tic!

Then it turned into to a driving rain.

Plop! Plop! Plop! Plop! Plop! Plop!

Which turned into a storm!

SPLASH! SPLASH! SPLASH! SPLASH!

IS IT A WALLABY OR A KANGAROO?

The wallaby is a marsupial of tiny dimensions. It can reach a height of 12 to 40 inches, while the red kangaroo can grow to 5 ½ feet tall. Kangaroos and wallabies can be found throughout Australia. They live in the desert and in wooded and rocky places.

kangaroo

wallaby

Paulina, Colette, Pam, and Violet had never seen rain like this! The falling drops were as big as cheese slices!

"I'm pulling over," Nicky declared. "I can't see past the tip of my snout. Plus, it's getting dark."

So they waited, and waited, and waited. But the rain just wouldn't let up.

Paulina brought out some Cheesy Chews and apple juice.

THE WOLLEMI PINE

Imagine sitting in the shade of a tree that was alive during the time of the dinosaurs. It can happen in Australia! On September 10, 1994, David Noble discovered a species of trees that was previously thought extinct, in a deep gorge in the Blue Mountains of New South Wales: the Wollemi pine. This particular conifer was alive 200 million years ago! The trees grow to a height of 130 feet and have narrow, tapered leaves. The Wollemi pine is one of the most protected trees on the planet.

"Thank goodness you packed snacks!" exclaimed Pam. "I'm hungrier than a rodent on a MouseFast diet."

After eating, sleep overtook the exhausted mouselings. One after the other, the five friends slipped into a peaceful slumber.

WHAT'S A BILLABONG?

A few hours later, the five friends woke to a tremendous racket. It was the song of a thousand birds.

"Ugh!" **Violet** moaned. She kept her eyes closed tight.

"What time is it?" PAULINA mumbled.

Pamela rubbed her stomach. "My tummy tells me it's breakfast time!"

But outside the SUV's windows, IT WAS STILL AS DARK AS MIDNIGHT.

Nicky rolled over, stretched, and yawned. Then she shouted, "Be quieeeeeeeet!"

Instantly, a hundred **brightly colored** wings fluttered and rose in flight. A moment later, **sunlight** shone through the **SUV**'s windows.

"What was that?" Violet cried, looking confused.

During the **NIGHT**, an incredible thing had occurred. Dozens of birds had covered the SUV. They had perched all over it: on the roof, on the doors, and on the hood until the entire vehicle was covered! That's why it seemed as dark as night when the mouselings looked out the windows.

The **Thea Sisters**

watched the birds as they **FLEW AWAY**.

"I've got to get a picture of this!" said Colette. She reached for the door handle and hopped out.

"**Eeeeeek!**" shrieked Colette. There was water everywhere!

Nicky reached over and helped her back in. "Are you OK, Colette?"

"*Do I look OK?!*" Colette screeched. "I just took a bath in a swamp!"

Violet grabbed a towel and wrapped it around her friend. Paulina offered her a sip of juice. After a few minutes, Colette was calm again.

Pam turned to Nicky. "What happened? How did we end up in a lake?"

"It's not a lake," Nicky explained. "It's a billabong. Billabongs are big puddles that form after rainstorms. They're not very deep, but they're enormouse!"

"Well if the water's shallow, then we can keep on driving," said Pam.

Nicky shook her snout. "It's too risky. We could drive into a huge pothole, and the SUV

could **sink**. Or there could be crocodiles."

"CROCODILES?!" Colette exclaimed.

Nicky nodded. "This is terrible! We're stuck here until help comes along. And the sheep are probably getting sicker by the minute. What do we do?"

Paulina put a paw around Nicky. She looked at the other mouselings for help. But no one knew what to do.

Then suddenly, Pamela leaped up. "Hey, Sisters!" she exclaimed. "What did that rodent from the car rental shop say?"

Colette frowned. "I think he said, 'This baby's got **EVERYTHING YOU NEED FOR AN ABSOLUTELY FABUMOUSE ADVENTURE!**'"

"Well then, it's time to put it to the test!" Pamela declared. And with that, she pushed open the ceiling hatch and climbed out onto the SUV's roof.

EVERYTHING YOU NEED FOR AN ABSOLUTELY FABUMOUSE ADVENTURE

"What are you doing out there?" Colette asked, sticking her snout through the hatch.

"There's a lot of gear in this roof rack!" Pam exclaimed as she dug through the bundle strapped to the SUV's roof. There was a **first aid kit**, a compass, and helmets.

"**Holey cheese!**" Pamela cried. "There's a **RAFT**! A real blow-up raft with oars!"

"You mean . . . you want us to **row** all the way to Nepabunna?" Violet asked

anxiously. "Through the **CROCODILES**?"

"Not all the way to Nepabunna," Pam reassured her. "Just to that MOUNTAIN."

Her friends looked at where Pam was pointing. It was not very far from the SUV.

"Great idea, Pam!" Nicky exclaimed. "That's Saint Mary's Peak, the highest MOUNTAIN in the Flinders Ranges. We can climb it. The billabong can't extend all the way to the other side, and there's a **ROAD** over there. We can get a ride to the nearest town."

Paulina and Violet were nodding. But Colette looked worried. "Are we going to have to climb with our **bare paws**?"

Pam just grinned. "No worries, Colette!" she said. "Look what I found." She pulled out ropes, nails, and crampons. The roof rack had everything they'd need for a MOUNTAIN CLIMB.

"EVERYTHING YOU NEED
FOR AN ABSOLUTELY
FABUMOUSE ADVENTURE!"

PINK IS MY
FAVORITE COLOR!

Pam, Nicky, Violet, Paulina, and Colette clambered into the raft. Pam steered it toward the MOUNTAIN. She was brimming with excitement. "Admit it, mouselings. We're paddling in a raft in the Outback and we're about to climb a famouse mountain. This has got to be our **greatest** adventure ever!"

Her enthusiasm was contagious. The sky was clear after the storm. The COOL air gave the mouselings a burst of energy.

"It feels good to **MOVE** my paws after so many hours sitting in planes, trains, and SUVs," said Paulina.

Everyone agreed. Well, almost **everyone**.

"I can't wait to get back to civilization,"

moaned Colette. "Just look at my fur! It's all matted and muddy."

"Colette, even on a bad fur day, you look a zillion times better than I do," said Violet. She pulled something out of the bottom of the raft. "Look! This *pink* helmet looks as if it was made just for you."

Colette put it on and smiled. "Pink *is* my favorite color!" She turned to **HUG** her friend. "Thanks, Violet. You're the best!"

About half an hour later, they reached the mountain. Pam had been **MOUNTAIN CLIMBING** a few times before, so she was in charge of checking everyone's equipment. As Nicky began to lead the mouselings up the mountain, Pam made them **DIZZY** with her advice.

"Never take off your helmet! Never take climbing lightly! Never climb during bad weather! Never underestimate a mountain! Never forget your first aid kit!"

Pam felt **RESPONSIBLE** for taking care of her friends. And Nicky, Colette, Paulina, and Violet felt responsible for rolling their **EYES** at all of her advice!

BETWEEN
WATER AND SKY

"One last **TRY**, Pam! You can do it! Come on, you're almost there!"

Violet was the first to make it to the top, with Paulina right behind her. Pamela couldn't believe those two had passed her. She gritted her teeth, curled up her tail, and **pulled** herself to the top.

"How — **huff! huff!** — did you do it?" she panted. She bent over to catch her breath. When she stood up, she gaped at the breathtaking panorama before her. "**INCREDIBLE!**"

"**STUPENDOUS!**" whispered Paulina.

"**Magnificent!**" Violet said, sighing.

"*Fabumouse!*" gasped Nicky.

"Moldy Brie balls, **MORE WATER**?!" cried Colette.

She was right! The billabong extended all the way to the other side of Saint Mary's Peak. It was **IMMENSE**. A forest of trees and rocky peaks peeped up from below the water's surface.

The mouselings were silent for a moment. They were awestruck by the sight before them. Then, in the distance, they saw an odd-looking vehicle approaching. It was a hydroplane — a boat that skims the water's surface. The boat was powered by a propeller that looked like an enormouse **FAN**!

Nicky jumped for joy when she saw it. "Kissing kangaroos! It's **Mitch**!"

Mitch was another of Naya's many grandchildren. He was a **TALL**, friendly mouse with a furdo of tightly knitted **BRAIDS**.

"I'm sure Doctor Ted put him on our **trail**," said Nicky. "Hooray! We're rescued!" She started waving frantically, trying to signal her cousin.

Nicky was right. Doctor Ted had radioed Mitch and asked him to look out for Nicky and her friends.

An hour later, the five **mouselings** were continuing their journey on board Mitch's hydroplane. The flooded landscape was surreal.

"I feel like I'm in a *dream*," Paulina said with a sigh.

Violet nodded. "And I don't ever want to wake up!"

As the *SUN*

Mitch, Nicky's cousin

began to set, the little group finally reached the end of the billabong — right on the edge of a **HIGHWAY**. "This is a good place to find a ride," Mitch said.

Pamela, Violet, Paulina, and Colette looked at one another in confusion. But they decided to wait to see what would happen.

After a few minutes, a dot appeared on the horizon.

"A camper!" said Paulina.

"It's covered with *flowers*!" noted Colette.

"It's Billy!" exclaimed Nicky.

THAT REALLY, REALLY HURTS!

In the meantime, Mortimer MacCardigan wasn't doing too well. After *plotting* to make Nicky and her friends lose their ride to Nepabunna, he demanded that **Nate** come with him.

"BUT WHERE ARE WE GOING?" asked Nate.

"To Nepabunna to find out what that nosy little rodent is up to!" Mortimer roared.

Just as they were about to get on their plane, Mortimer *tripped* on a rock and sprained an ankle.

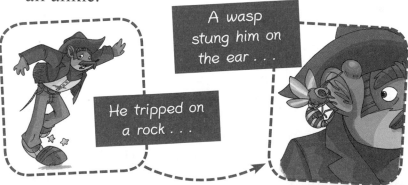

A wasp stung him on the ear . . .

He tripped on a rock . . .

He crushed his paw in the window . . .

And he caught a terrible cold!

"Ouch!" Mortimer cried. **"That hurts!"**

Then, a wasp flew through the window and stung him on the ear.

"Ouch! That hurts!" Mortimer exclaimed. **"It really, really hurts!"**

He decided to close the window and **crushed** his paw in it.

"Ouch! That hurts!" Mortimer screeched. **"It really, really, hurts!"**

Then the same storm that had hit Nicky and her friends struck as Mortimer and Nate MacCardigan were in flight. The plane jolted and **BOUNCED UP AND DOWN**, giving

Mortimer a collection of **LUMPS** on his snout.

To top it all off, the **STORM** got so bad that they had to make an emergency landing for the night. The raindrops PELTED the plane so loudly, the two mice hardly got a wink of sleep.

The next morning, Mortimer's ankle was puffy and swollen. His ear was **throbbing**. His paw ached. His snout was covered with **LUMPS** and **BUMPS**. And he had caught a **terrible cold**!

"Dad, let's just go home," Nate pleaded.

But the thought of giving up made Mortimer angrier than the wasp that had stung him.

"Shut your snout, Nate!" Mortimer snapped "We'll do nothing of the sort!"

Mortimer was acting like a **TOUGH MOUSE**, but the truth was, he really needed to see a doctor.

"Let's go to Curdimurka," Nate suggested. "There will be tons of rodents there for the Outback Ball. There's sure to be a *doctor* who can check you out."

"Hmpf," Mortimer snorted. "That's not a bad idea, Nate. I guess the **CHeese** doesn't fall too far from the CRACKER after all."

Nate just rolled his eyes. He loved his dad, but he could be a real **PaiN** in the **tail**.

WELCOME TO CURDIMURKA!

Curdimurka was home to many settlers during the construction of the Ghan northern railway in the late 1800s. After the railroad was completed, the town fell into disrepair. Nowadays, Curdimurka comes alive every two years during the Outback Ball, an event that attracts thousands of people.

THE MOST ELEGANT MOUSE AT THE OUTBACK BALL!

Billy helped the mouselings into the camper. Then he told them some bad **news**.

"All the streets are **blocked**," he announced. "We have to spend the night in Curdimurka. **Tonight** is the night of the Outback Ball. And sick sheep or no sick sheep, you shouldn't miss it!"

"*The Outback Ball?*" Colette asked. "What's that?"

"Every two years, the Outback Ball takes place in Curdimurka," explained Nicky. "It's a traditional celebration that's very popular."

As they approached Curdimurka, they saw tons of rodents **crowding** the **STREETS**.

Everyone wanted to be part of the Outback Ball. Everyone except Nicky. She was thinking of her sick sheep and how she had to find a cure in a **hurry**. She didn't want to lose another second.

Violet could tell her friend was **DISTRESSED**. So she leaned in close. "There's an old Chinese proverb that goes like this: *If you can't go where you want, stay where you are.*"

Nicky looked at her, puzzled.

"You're here now and you can't do anything

about it," Violet explained. "So try to enjoy it!"

Nicky nodded slowly. **Violet** was right. The only thing to do was to enjoy today and continue on their journey tomorrow.

"*Okay, let's have a good time!*" said Nicky. They hopped out of the camper, and she began showing her friends around.

What an incredible place! There was *music* everywhere. There were **contests**, carousels, TOYS, and GAMES. And there were **hundreds** of different delicious things to **eat**.

The five mouselings were quickly drawn into the excitement. They were all *squeaking* at once, pointing at the booths they wanted to visit. Only Colette was quiet.

"Are you OK, *Colette*?" asked Nicky. "You look a little down in the snout."

At that, Colette broke down. "No, I'm **NOT** OK! I can't go to a ball like this! I look like I went **SWIMMING** in a **SWAMP**!"

"That's because you did," muttered Violet. Paulina giggled, but then quickly clamped a paw over her mouth.

"Listen, Colette," Nicky said seriously, "I gave you my word that if there was a dance, I'd worry about your *clothes*. So *snout up*! I'm a rodent of my word."

Nicky smiled at her friend. Then she JUMPED on a van that was parked nearby and yelled at the top of her lungs, "**Hey, rodents!**"

Nicky had quite a squeak! Everyone stopped talking and turned to look at her.

"My friend is here from a **faaaaaraway** place. She comes from France!"

A murmur passed through the crowd. "From France?"

Nicky had to **shout** again. "Yes, *France*—the fashion capital of the world! So you can understand how upset this lovely mouscling is that she doesn't have anything to wear to the ball. Let's show her true Australian hospitality! She needs pink clothes! Understand? Pink!"

There was a moment of silence as that sank in. Then the competition began.

"I have a pink jacket!" shouted a young rodent.

jacket

scarf

shawl

skirt

hat

belt

jewelry

"Is a RHINESTONE belt okay?" asked a tiny mouseling.

"I've got a shawl!" cried an older mouse.

A kind rat hawking cheese sticks offered his camper as a dressing room. Colette gladly accepted. She knew just what she needed to do first: WASH her fur! Then her friends helped her pick out **THE PERFECT LOOK**.

"Darling, you look ABSOLUTELY FABUMOUSE!" cried Nicky.

Colette beamed. "Thanks, Nicky!"

The ball began, and it was a blast! Nicky, Pam, Violet, Paulina, and Colette danced the night away, moving to the rhythm of a thousand different beats.

Around midnight, Violet looked around her. In all the CONFUSION, she had lost her friends! She tried calling to them, but it was too noisy. She tried looking for them, but it was too CROWDED.

Violet felt lost, lost, lost, lost! As she frantically searched through the sea of mice around her, the crowd began to move like a wave. Then everyone burst into applause.

Violet had no idea what was happening — until she heard a booming squeak over the loudsqueaker. "Come one, come all! It's time to award the prize for the *best-dressed* rodent at the ball!"

"Who do you think it will be?" someone near Violet asked.

"It's got to be that cute blond mouseling from France!" answered another.

"She's the most stylish rodent I've ever seen!"

"Oh, that's right, the one dressed all in pink," the first mouse said.

"You mean Colette!" exclaimed Violet. "But where is she?"

She got her answer a moment later. Colette was scurrying onstage to collect her prize!

"That's my friend!" cried Violet as she made her way through the crowd.

Rodents moved aside to let her through.

Violet was **RELIEVED** to find *Nicky*, PAULINA, *Pamela*, and **Billy** standing right in front of the stage. Everyone was clapping wildly. Colette was as beautiful as a *movie mouse*!

Other **prizes** were given out, too. Pam was voted the **most popular** rodent at the ball. Nicky got the prize for the **sportiest**. And Paulina took lots of photos. It was a night to remember!

Click!
Click!

A SPECIAL
TREATMENT

Mortimer MacCardigan had spent the night in Curdimurka, too. But instead of dancing the night away, he'd been recovering in the first aid clinic.

"Are you the one with a sprained ankle?" a doctor asked him.

"**Yesssss**," groaned Mortimer.

The doctor consulted his clipboard. "And the one with the ear *INFECTION*, the swollen paw, and the concussion?"

"Uh-huh," Mortimer moaned.

"*And* the one with the COLD?"

"Yes, that's me," Mortimer whimpered.

"Hmm," said the doctor, nodding thoughtfully. "You need massive treatment!"

Mortimer turned a delicate shade of green —
like **MOLD** on aged cheddar.

"Rosie!" the doctor called to the nurse
in the next room. "The patient we've been
waiting for is here. You know, the one who
needs **special treatment**!"

"W-what's special treatment?" stammered
Mortimer MacCardigan.

Rosie the nurse

Before the doctor could
answer, Rosie bustled in.
"Let's see . . . **aha**! What
you need is a **SHOT**! In
fact, two shots! Oh, what
the heck, let's make it
three shots!"

She pulled out an
ENORMOUS syringe and
a **loooooooooong**
needle! Mortimer took one

look and started planning his **ESCAPE**.

"Uh, on second thought, I'm feeling better. Much, much better. So I don't think I'll need the special, uh, treatment after all."

Rosie *laughed*. "**Afraid?** It's just these three shots, and then lots of fluids for your cold. So shut your snout and stop *fussing!*"

Mortimer MacCardigan was too terrified to argue anymore. A few hours later, he was sound asleep. His son, Nate, sat by his side, **WIDE-AWAKE**. He was too worried to sleep. He didn't like his father's behavior. It was wrong, **ALL WRONG**! But what could he do? Whenever he tried to protest, his father just **SHOUTED** him down.

Nate sighed. He was glad that the nurse had taken charge. He wished he had the **COURAGE** to stand up to his father the way she had.

Wistfully, Nate looked out the window.

He could hear the music and the laughter of the *celebration* in the city below. It felt very far away. He thought of Nicky. How **FUN** it would be to go to the ball with a mouse like her! He had no idea Nicky was just a couple of pawsteps away from him.

The next morning, **Mortimer MacCardigan** was back to his usual gruff self. He woke up Nate with a jolt and, without so much as a good morning, they boarded their plane and **TOOK OFF**.

DESTINATION: NEPABUNNA!

WE'RE VERY, VERY, VERY SLEEPY!

A few yards from the clinic, in front of Curdimurka's train station, you could hear music of a sort: *zzzz . . . zzzz . . . zzzzz . . . zzzzz . . . zzzz . . . zzzz . . . zzzz . . . zzzz . . . zzzz . . .*

It was a concert of snores. Pamela, Violet, Colette, Paulina, and Billy were sound asleep. So were dozens of other rodents. Everyone was counting sheep. But Nicky was wide-awake. Her head was filled with thoughts of her sheep, her parents, and the ranch that was in danger of being lost forever.

In the station's lobby, Billy was snoozing away. Nicky shook him gently by the tail. She wanted to leave as soon as possible. But Billy didn't move.

Colette woke up and tried to help her. She shouted in Billy's ear, "*Yoohoo! Billy!*"

"Ssshhhhhh!" said Paulina, covering her eyes with her paws. "**WE'RE VERY SLEEPY!**"

Colette tried to be quiet, but it wasn't easy. "*Hey, Billy!*" she whispered. "Wake up!"

Nicky kept trying to rouse her friends, but Paulina, Violet, and Pamela **COMPLAINED**, "We're too sleepy!"

Nicky was starting to get impatient. "Wake up! Wake up! **WAAAAAAKE UUUUPP!**"

That did it. Paulina, Pam, and Violet sprang to their paws and gathered their bags.

As for Billy, nothing seemed to work. So the five mouselings **picked him up** and **LOADED** him into the camper.

"OK, let's go!" Nicky said. "Colette, you're in charge of the **ROAD MAP**. We're off to Nepabunna!"

She carefully turned on the engine. She didn't want to disturb anyone.

VROOOOOOOOOOOOOOOMMMMM!

All around the station, sleepers woke up.

"Shh!" one shouted.

"We're very sleepy!" cried another.

"Oops!" said Nicky. "Sorry about that!"

But almost before she finished squeaking, they were all asleep again. At least, for a moment. There was another loud **VROOOOOM**, and the sleepers picked up their snouts again.

"Shhhhh!" one shouted.

"We're **very sleepy**!" cried another.

"It wasn't me this time, I swear!" she cried. "That sound came from up there!" She pointed to the sky. As she did, she recognized the plane that was taking off.

It was **Mortimer MacCardigan**!

WELCOME TO NEPABUNNA!

When Nicky saw that plane, she became even more determined to get to Nepabunna. She raced out of Curdimurka at *top speed*. Until . . .

putt... PUtt... PUTT... PUMPF!

The camper came to a dead stop. It had run out of gas!

Nicky was so **anxious** to get to Nepabunna, she had forgotten to check the tank. "Argh! What a DRONGO!" she cried.

"What is she talking about?" Violet whispered to Paulina.

"I think it's Australian for 'idiot,'" Paulina whispered back.

"Of all the **stupid** things I've ever done,

this is the **stupidest!**" Nicky continued.

Billy chose that moment to wake up at last. "Huh? Where are we?"

"We're **HALFWAY** to Nepabunna and we ran out of gas!" cried Nicky.

"There must be a gas station along the way," volunteered *Pamela*. "I'll scamper off, get a gallon, and come right back."

"Good idea," Billy said, yawning. "I think there may be one about **FIFTEEN MILES** away."

"Fifteen miles?" said Pam, **frowning**. "There isn't one any closer?"

Nicky was in despair. The rest of the **Thea Sisters** tried to comfort her.

"It's going to be OK, Nic," Paulina said. "We'll think of something."

Billy chose that exact moment to think of something **SMART**. He grabbed the radio. "**Mitch!** We need you!"

Half an hour later, Mitch arrived in his jeep to **RESCUE** them!

Billy filled the tank with extra gas Mitch kept in his backseat. Then he said good-bye to Nicky and her friends and headed back to the ranch. Mitch would drive the mouselings to Nepabunna.

Nicky sighed with relief. Her mission was almost over! In a little while, she'd meet Naya's C L A N E L D E R S. She was sure they'd know a cure for the sheep.

Soon, the paved road turned into a **PATH**. They were getting closer!

The mouselings had to proceed on paw, along with a thick **CLOUD** of flies, horseflies, gadflies, tiger mosquitoes, gnats, wasps, bees, and **GIGANTIC** hornets.

Clue!

Besides parrots, insects, and koalas, who else is keeping an eye on the Thea Sisters? Can you find them?

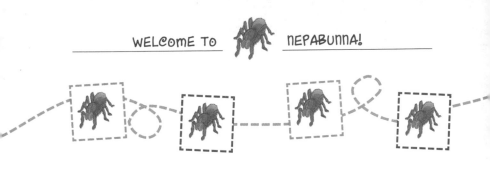
Suddenly, some **ABORIGINE MOUSELINGS** appeared. Their hair and bodies were covered with dried **mud**.

"Hmm," said Colette. "I wonder if it's a fashion statement?"

Mitch laughed. "Not exactly! But the **mud** does serve a purpose. It protects these little mice from **insect bites** and **SUNBURNS**."

Together the mouselings greeted the park ranger. "Hi, Uncle Mitch!"

"They're Naya's great-great-grandchildren,"

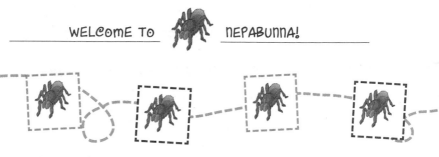

Mitch explained to the **Thea Sisters**.

"Are all Australians related to you?" asked Pamela incredulously.

Mitch just laughed. "No, but it seems that way sometimes!"

The kids greeted the Thea Sisters in chorus: "Hello, strangers with odd-looking snouts, you look really far out!"

Then they scampered off, laughing.

Pamela shivered. She'd realized the Aborigine mouselings were running after enormouse **HAIRY SPIDERS**!

Violet knew Pamela was afraid of insects.

"**Don't worry**," whispered Violet, taking Pam's paw. "I'll protect you!"

A MYSTERIOUS
CLUE

Mitch and the Thea Sisters followed the Aborigine mouselings' path. Twenty minutes later, they reached the Aborigines' camp.

NAYA's message had already reached the camp, so the mouselings were expected. It was dinnertime, and the delicious **SMELL** of cheese stew made their mouths water.

"Hurrah!" cried Pam. "**WE'RE EATING!**" The mouselings fell on the stew like a pack of **hungry** field mice.

A young Aborigine mouse came and greeted the Thea Sisters. She was short and slender and wore a beautiful flowered dress.

"This is my fiancée, **Lily**," Mitch said.

"It's great to meet you, Lily!" said Nicky.

"But where are the CLAN'S ELDERS?"

"They are AWAY on an important journey," Lily said. "I'm not sure when they'll be back."

Nicky was crushed. "But I have to talk with them! I came hundreds of miles to meet them!" It was all she could do not to start sobbing like a tiny mouseling.

"UNFORTUNATELY, I can't tell you where they are," Lily said sympathetically. It's a secret place that only members of the clan can visit."

"But my grandmother is a member of the clan," Nicky protested.

"I'm very sorry, Nicky," said Lily. "But it's not for me to decide."

LILY

A **tear** trickled down Nicky's snout. Violet quickly pulled her aside. "The necklace! Show her the necklace Naya gave you!"

With **EVERYTHING** that had happened, Nicky had forgotten all about the necklace. "Look!" she said. "My grandmother gave this to me!"

Lily gazed at the necklace in surprise. "I'm so glad you showed this to me, Nicky! This **medallion** means that you are a trusted member of our clan. It changes everything."

"Hooray!" cried Paulina.

"The elders have gone to **Uluru**, the **GREAT RED ROCK**," Lily said.

"I know Uluru!" exclaimed Nicky. "It's a **famouse** Australian **LANDMARK**."

AUSTRALIA

Uluru

"To see the elders, you have to find the mountain inside the mountain," **Lily** explained. She pointed to the desert mouse carved in Naya's necklace. **"This will show you the way."**

"I don't get it," Nicky said. "How?"

"Don't worry," Lily reassured her. "When the time comes, you'll understand."

While Lily and Nicky were talking, Pamela was *rummaging* through her backpack.

"SQUEEEEEEEEAK!" Pamela shrieked. She had touched an **ENORMOUSE HAIRY SPIDER**! She turned the backpack inside out, and the spider ran away. It quickly scurried into the **WOODS**.

A moment later, they heard another shriek.

SQUEEEAK!!

"Squeeeeeeeeak! Get it off me!"
It was **Mortimer MacCardigan**!
He'd been busy spying on Nicky when the
ENORMOUSE HAIRY SPIDER jumped

right on his snout. Nicky,
Paulina, Colette, Violet, and
Pamela watched as Mortimer
scampered away with his
tail between his legs.

DANGEROUS SPIDERS

Australia is home to many of the
world's deadliest spiders, including
the Atrax robustus, commonly known as the
Sydney funnel web. It is a tiny, dark spider
that weaves funnel-shaped webs around its
burrows in order to trap prey. These funnel
web spiders live under damp rocks and logs
within a hundred miles of Sydney.

didgeridoo

THE JOURNEY
BEGINS AGAIN

Night was falling. The mouselings settled in to spend the night. But try as she might, Nicky could not **FALL ASLEEP**. She checked and rechecked her map. The distance from Nepabunna to **Kuru** looked **IMMENSE**.

"Something is worrying her," Lily said.

Paulina quickly explained about Nicky's sheep. "She's afraid she won't be in time!" she concluded. "Her sheep need medicine right now!"

As soon as she heard this, Lily pointed to a long, hollow eucalyptus branch. It was decorated with a thousand COLORED DOTS.

"Oh! I know what that is!" Pamela said. "It's called a *giggiridu*!"

"Actually, it's a *didgeridoo*!" Mitch corrected her. He grabbed the instrument and blew forcefully into it. The didgeridoo **vibrated**, emitting a low, powerful sound.

MMHOUUUU-IUUU-OUUU-IUUU-OUUU.

A few moments later, another didgeridoo answered like a distant echo.

Mitch was using the didgeridoo to communicate! He turned to Nicky. "I found you a ride! You'll leave tomorrow morning on **DOCTOR TED**'s plane."

Nicky threw her paws around her cousin. "Thank you, Mitch! Thank you so much!"

With her heart at peace at last, Nicky quickly fell into a sound sleep. So did the other mouselings. They were all exhausted from their long day of traveling.

The next morning, the entire clan showed up to wish the **Thea Sisters** well. The Aborigine mouselings sang to them once more: "*Hello, strangers with odd-looking snouts, you look really far out!!*"

Mitch and Lily took the mouselings to the nearest landing strip. DOCTOR TED was already there waiting for them.

Nicky gave Mitch and Lily each a big hug. All five mouselings thanked their new friends.

"You really make a **great couple**!" Pam told Mitch and Lily.

"Thank you so much for all your help, and for your friendship," Violet said *sincerely*.

"True friends are truly **precious**!" said Lily, smiling.

true friends are
truly precious!

LiKE FONDUE
iN A PoT!

As their plane *zoomed* toward Uluru, Nicky peered out the window. She knew that Mortimer MacCardigan was following them. He knew where they were headed, and she was sure they hadn't seen the last of him. What Nicky didn't know was that Mortimer had already arrived at **Uluru**. And he had planned a trap for her and her friends! But something had happened to disrupt his plans. Something **REALLY BIG**!

That morning, Mortimer was complaining about Nicky as usual. "I'll teach that busymouse a lesson or two!"

Poor **Nate** was drinking a cup of **HOT CHEDDAR**, trying to wake up. He slept in

Uluru

Mortimer MacCardigan

the nose of the plane and he had woken up with his tail tied in **knots**.

Mortimer continued ranting and raving. "That **NOSY LITTLE MOUSELING** sent that **ENORMOUSE** spider my way on purpose! Well I'll **show** her! I'll have my **REVENGE**! I'll —"

Nate couldn't bear it a moment longer. "That's it, Dad," he said. **"I'VE HAD IT.** Count me **OUT**!"

It was the first time

Nate had ever **disobeyed** his father!

But Mortimer MacCardigan was *furious*. He stamped his paws. He screamed at Nate. He tore at his fur.

But it was no use. Nate just put his paws over his ears and pretended he couldn't hear. **THEN HE TURNED AND LEFT.**

Soon Mortimer was all alone at the foot of **Kkuru**.

It was **HOT**. It was **TOO HOT**! Mortimer was as hot as fondue in a pot!

He decided to seek shelter in the shade of a rock. "Maybe I'll rest a little," he thought.

A few moments later, he was fast asleep.

THE MOUNTAIN
OF FIRE

The **Thea Sisters** reached Uluru when the sun was still high in the sky. **Doctor Ted** had received an urgent call, so he said good-bye and quickly took off again.

Nicky wiped the sweat from her snout. "It's **TOO HOT**!" she said. "We'd better wait until the **sun** goes down. Let's rest a little."

The mouselings dropped their packs in the **shade** and sat down.

"Look at this rock!" Colette gushed. "It's amazing!"

As the girls squeaked away, Nicky kept thinking about **Lily's** mysterious words. She couldn't make **snouts** or **tails** of them. *"Look for the mountain inside the*

mountain. It will show you the way."

Nicky took out Naya's necklace and gazed at the medallion of the desert mouse. How could IT show her the way? Try as she might, she just couldn't figure it out.

Finally, the sun dipped low over the horizon. Uluru looked more imposing and MYstERIOUs than ever. In the light of dusk, it looked like a mountain of fire!

Nicky pulled out a pair of binoculars and began examining the many grooves and gorges on Uluru. She was hoping to find a passageway into the mountain. She didn't realize that another pair of EYES was

watching *her* through binoculars. It was **Nate MacCardigan**! The young mouseling had begun tracking the five friends. He was worried about them.

On one side of the mountain, Nicky found a **CRACK** big enough for a small rodent to fit through. She handed the binoculars to Paulina. "Take a look. Maybe the passage into the mountain is through that crack."

PAULINA studied the crack with the binoculars for a long time. "It could be. But how do we know which is the right crack?"

"Lily said the mouse on the necklace would show you the way," Pamela said.

Violet was taking a turn with the binoculars. She **focused** them on one crack after another, noticing some odd-looking markings. She focused again.

"Cheese dumplings with soy sauce!"

Violet cried, passing the binoculars back to **Nicky**. "Do you see what I see?"

Nicky **LOOKED**. A moment later, she opened her eyes in surprise. The place Violet had indicated was covered with ancient Aborigine painting! There were wavy lines, spirals, turtles, lizards, eagles, and *SNAKES*. But above all, there were **lots and lots and lots** of desert mice just like the one carved on Naya's necklace!

There are a lot of designs of desert mice on this part of Uluru. Do you see anything unusual about their tails?

Uluru, once known as Ayers Rock, is the tip of a rocky outcrop of sandstone that stretches underground for many miles.

Uluru is 1,132 feet tall and about 6 miles around at its base. Aboveground, it is more than 2 miles long, 1 mile wide, and oval in shape.

The wind and rain have carved many gorges on Uluru. On days when the wind is strong, the gorges "moan" in a very mysterious way. This phenomenon has given rise to many legends.

Uluru sits in the middle of terrain that is completely flat. The best times to visit the site are at sunrise and sunset, when the light of the sun makes the rock glow red.

Uluru is a sacred site to the Aborigines, with cave paintings that date back thousands of years.

THE TAILS
HAVE IT!

"Let's go check it out," Paulina suggested. "If we see those **desert** mice up close, maybe we'll find a clue to the way in."

Nicky and her friends began hiking toward the sacred mountain, heading in the direction of the rodent paintings. Soon the side covered with painting was just above them. And Paulina was right — there were lots of *little mice*!

The mouselings examined them **closely**.

"This one has a curved tail,"

Pamela said.

"This one has a straight tail,"

Violet pointed out. "This one has an arrow tail," observed Colette. "Just like the one on the medallion."

Nicky and Paulina came closer to take a better look.

"You're absolutely right!" said Paulina. "Good for you, Colette!"

"Maybe we should try following the **direction** the arrow-tailed mice are pointing," Nicky said slowly. "Perhaps they'll be the ones to show us the way!"

Violet clapped her paws together. "What a fabumouse idea!"

"That's it, Nic," Paulina squeaked, squeezing her friend's paw. "I'm sure of it. You **figured it out**!" She looked down. There was a

rough-looking path on the **ground** right in front of them. "Look!"

"A passage between the rocks!" **CRIED** Nicky.

The setting sun **LIT** a tiny crack that opened into the rocks right where the desert mice were pointing. The mouselings felt their ears **quiver** with anticipation.

"Well, what are we waiting for?" Pamela asked. "Let's go!"

One by one, the five friends squeezed into the crack and scurried along the path. After turning a corner, they found themselves in front of another crack in the **ROCK**. It led to a very narrow and dark passageway.

"**UXURU** is a **SACRED MOUNTAIN**," Violet said uncertainly. "Maybe it's not right to go any farther."

"But we're not being disrespectful!" Pamela protested.

"**OF COURSE NOT!**" said Nicky, touching the necklace. "We are on a *MISSION*, and this medallion is proof of our good faith. Naya

told us it would protect us. Let's go in and find the elders!"

The five friends held **paws** for a moment. "Friends together! Mice forever!"

Nicky took a deep breath, then grabbed the FLASHLIGHT and slid into the dark passageway. One after another, her friends followed her.

THE MOUNTAIN INSIDE THE MOUNTAIN

The passageway sloped deep underground into the heart of the mountain. As the mouselings crept carefully along, the ground beneath their paws became steeper and **more slippery**.

Suddenly, something moved in the shadows.

"**WHAT'S THAT?!**" cried Pamela.

Nicky pointed her flashlight toward one wall of the passage. It was covered with **ENORMOUSE**, **GIGANTIC** *millipedes*!

"**Squeeeeeeeeak!**" Pamela shouted.

Nicky, Paulina, Violet, and Colette gathered around to protect her.

"Don't WORRY, Pam!" Colette said.

"Remember, friends together, mice forever!" Violet said.

Once Pamela had calmed down, the five mouselings continued on their way. The tunnel became narrower and narrower. It was giving Nicky the chills. She couldn't stand tight spaces.

Paulina held her friend's paw. "Just a little farther, Nicky!"

Nicky, Paulina, Colette, Violet, and Pamela continued scurrying along the narrow underground tunnel. They had NO CLUE where it would take them.

"I feel like a rat in a maze," Pam said.

"Me, too," said **Violet**. "I'm EXHAUSTED. I can't go on much farther."

"It's just a **little** farther," said Paulina encouragingly. "Come on, mouselings! We can do it!"

Just then, the tunnel ended. The mouselings found themselves in a huge, dark cave lit only by a few small fires. Some Aborigines were gathered around each one. Their snouts were *decorated* with white and yellow paint.

The five mouselings were squeakless. So this was the mountain inside the mountain! They stood as still as **STONES**, taking it all in.

Then they heard a rodent behind them.

"Hello, **STRANGERS**! Are you looking for something?"

They turned to see three Aborigines. All three were old, with long white fur TIED IN KNOTS on top of their heads.

"I'm Boba," said the first.

Louisa

Napa

Boba

"I'm *Louisa*," said the second.

"I'm Napa," said the third.

"It's very **NiCe** to meet all three of you," said Nicky. "We came all this way to talk to the WISE ELDERS of my grandmother Naya's clan. Can you point them out to us?"

Boba laughed. "No need to point."

Napa nodded. "We're the elders!"

Louisa **gestured** to the closest fire. "Come tell us why you have come."

Boba offered the mouselings some delicious-smelling soup. As they ate, *Nicky* showed the elders her necklace and told them all about her quest.

"Naya told me there is a root that heals all illnesses, even **LEAD** poisoning. And she said you could help me find it."

The three wise ones looked at one another and started to **laugh**.

"I'm sorry, my dear," said Boba. "We don't mean to laugh at you. It's just that the root has been with you all the time." He pointed to Nicky's necklace.

Nicky couldn't believe her ears. "I'm afraid I don't understand."

"THIS NECKLACE IS MADE WITH THE ROOT YOU ARE SEEKING,"

Napa explained.

This **news** left the mouselings squeakless.

"I can't believe we came all this way for something we've had all along!" Colette finally exclaimed.

Pam nodded. "But wasn't it a fabumouse ADVENTURE?"

Louisa told Nicky what to do to help her sheep. "Take some seeds from the necklace and cook them. A few should be enough for twenty-five gallons of WATER. Let the mixture boil very slowly for three hours. If you want, you can add a *pinch* of cheese. Your sheep will love it!"

"Thank you!" said Nicky. "Thank you so much!" She turned back to her friends. "OK, **LET'S GO**, Mouselings! The sheep are waiting for us."

But at that very second, a **FRANTIC SHRIEK** echoed through the cavern.

OUCH! OUCH! OUCH!

Who was it? Who let out that desperate cry? Why, Mortimer MacCardigan, of course!

When Mortimer was last seen, he was at the foot of Uluru, seeking shelter in the **SHADOW** of a rock. The intense heat had overwhelmed him, and he'd fallen asleep. He slept deeply, dreaming he was the biggest sheep breeder in all of Australia.

In fact, in his dream, he was the biggest sheep breeder in the entire **WORLD**!

Millions and millions and millions of sheep surrounded him!

But a **strange** thing happened to Mortimer MacCardigan after he nodded off. He started SLEEPWALKING! He got

Mortimer MacCardigan, the biggest sheep breeder in the world!

up and began scampering up the ridge to **Uluru**.

Eyes shut tight, Mortimer put one paw in front of the other. He scurried along a narrow path with his paws out in front of him. Soon he was deep inside the **ROCK**.

As he crept along, his head banged on a **CRACK** in the rock. "Ouch! That really hurts!"

Mortimer woke with a start and realized he couldn't see a thing! It was PITCH-BLACK inside the rock. By accident, he grabbed a **very thorny** bush.

"Ouch! That really, really hurts!"

Mortimer jumped away from the bush. But he didn't realize he was right on the **EDGE** of a steep gorge! He fell into it, howling, "Ouch! Ouch! Ouch! That really, really, really hurts! Help!"

And that was the shout the **Thea Sisters** and the elders heard!

Nate MacCardigan had been secretly following *Nicky* and her friends. When he heard his father's cry of pain, he scurried out of his hiding place. He was determined to help his father.

FiVE SPECiAL NECKLACES!

Nate ran into the elders' cave. "Nicky!" he gasped. "What my father did to you was **wrong**, and I am so sorry! But please, in the name of our old friendship, please help me. My father's stuck in a gorge. Will you help me pull him out?"

Nicky didn't think twice. She grabbed a rope and looked at Boba, Napa, and Louisa. She was silently asking their permission. The three WISE ONES smiled and nodded.

Nate and Nicky *rushed* through the PASSAGEWAYS, heading toward Mortimer MacCardigan.

Getting to Mortimer turned out to be easy. The HARD PART was convincing

him to let Nicky help!

"I don't **trust** that busymouse!" Mortimer shrieked. "She'll help pull me up and then she'll drop me **FLAT** on my snout!"

"She won't, Dad," Nate said. "She only wants to help you, I swear."

Nicky nodded. "**Nate's right**, Mr. MacCardigan."

Eventually, Mortimer MacCardigan gave in. Nate and Nicky tossed the rope down to him, and he grabbed it.

Then he, Nate, and Nicky pulled with all their STRENGTH. Moments later, Mortimer MacCardigan was safe.

Nate and his father hugged.

Then Nicky, Nate, and Mortimer headed back to the cave, where the elders and Nicky's friends were waiting anxiously. When they saw Nicky was safe, they let out a cheer.

Now it really was time for good-byes. The wise ones gave the **Thea Sisters** five special necklaces — symbols of eternal friendship.

Colette fastened hers around her neck right away. "I'm never going to take it off," she declared. "Something like this never goes out of style!"

Louisa squeezed *Nicky*'s paw and said, "Go now, little one. Your sheep need you!"

A ROSE FOR NICKY!

The **Thea Sisters** hurried back to the ranch. No sooner had they arrived than Nicky and Naya whipped up a batch of seed soup. The sheep loved it! Within a few days, their **wool** began to grow in, **THICK** and **LUXURIOUS**. The sheep could enter the Grand Shearing contest, and Naya could sell the wool. the ranch was saved!

Nicky, Paulina, Colette, Pamela, and Violet took turns telling Naya the tale of their fabumouse adventure to **NEPABUNNA**.

Nicky's parents called, and Nicky filled them in. Her father and mother couldn't wait to see Nicky and to meet her extraordinary friends.

Naya hugged Nicky. "I'm **proud** of you!"

"It was all because of your necklace, **NAYA**!" answered Nicky as she gave it back to her grandmother.

Naya shook her snout, smiling. "You mean *your* necklace, my little cheese dumpling! This belongs to you now! You've earned it!"

Nicky's eyes filled with tears.

Naya threw a **huge party** to celebrate the sheep's recovery. She cooked all day to prepare the feast. She even asked a band, the **DesErt Mice**, to come play.

The Desert Mice

THE BIG PARTY AT THE RANCH!

Violet played the violin.

Pamela accompanied her with clapsticks.

Colette sang.

Paulina sang, too.

Nicky showed off her horseback-riding skills!

Practically everyone the **Thea Sisters** had met during their adventure was invited: Doctor Ted, Lily and Mitch, and Billy in his *flowered* camper.

Violet played the violin, while Pamela accompanied her on clapsticks. Paulina and Colette sang. For the grand finale, Nicky performed some acrobatic tricks on horseback. It was truly FABUMOUSE!

At midnight, the partygoers heard a

plane flying over the farm. It came closer and closer.

It was **Mortimer MacCardigan**! And he was lowering a **big barrel** over the side.

"Not again!" Nicky gasped.

The barrel touched the ground gently and **rolled** in front of the band.

The **Desert Mice** stopped playing. For a moment, no one moved. Everyone just *stared* at the **barrel**.

Finally, Nicky went

to check it out. A note from **Mortimer MacCardigan** was attached to one side.

Dear Nicky,

I'm sorry I tried to hurt your ranch. The truth is, I was jealous of your sheep. Now I understand I was in the wrong. Please accept this gift for your party. I hope one day you can forgive me.

Mortimer
MacCardigan

Nicky smiled and peered inside the barrel. It was full of **CHEESE**! Everyone **laughed**.

Attached to the barrel was a *red rose* with a note: *To Nicky from Nate.*

As she smelled it, Nicky turned **red** from the tip of her snout to the tip of her tail. Her friends winked at one another. "**WHAT A HEARTBREAKER YOU ARE, NIC!**" Colette exclaimed.

A moment later, the band was playing again. Nicky, Violet, Paulina, Pamela, and Colette all scampered onto the dance floor and started *shaking* their tails. They danced until the moon was low in the sky and the sun began to peek over the horizon.

As the sun rose, the fabumouse Australian exploits of the **Thea Sisters** came to an end. It was an **ADVENTURE** none of the mouselings would ever forget.

The next day, the five friends left for **MOUSEFORD ACADEMY**. It was time

to get back to their real life. They had to study and take **FINALS**.

But even their exams didn't **SCARE** them, because they were together and because they were *friends*.

They were more than friends. They were sisters!

THEA SISTERS

Thea Stilton

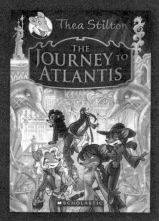

Secret Fairies

Don't miss any of these exciting series featuring the Thea Sisters!

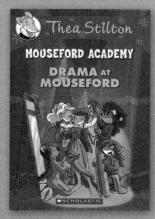

Treasure Seekers

Mouseford Academy

Don't miss any of these exciting Thea Sisters adventures!

Thea Stilton and the
Dragon's Code

Thea Stilton and the
Mountain of Fire

Thea Stilton and the
Ghost of the Shipwreck

Thea Stilton and the
Secret City

Thea Stilton and the
Mystery in Paris

Thea Stilton and the
Cherry Blossom Adventure

Thea Stilton and the
Star Castaways

Thea Stilton: Big Trouble
in the Big Apple

Thea Stilton and the
Ice Treasure

Thea Stilton and the
Secret of the Old Castle

Thea Stilton and the
Blue Scarab Hunt

Thea Stilton and the
Prince's Emerald

Thea Stilton and the
Mystery on the Orient Express

Thea Stilton and the
Dancing Shadows

Thea Stilton and the
Legend of the Fire Flowers

Thea Stilton and the
Spanish Dance Mission

**Thea Stilton and the
Journey to the Lion's Den**

**Thea Stilton and the
Great Tulip Heist**

**Thea Stilton and the
Chocolate Sabotage**

**Thea Stilton and the
Missing Myth**

**Thea Stilton and the
Lost Letters**

**Thea Stilton and the
Tropical Treasure**

**Thea Stilton and the
Hollywood Hoax**

**Thea Stilton and the
Madagascar Madness**

**Thea Stilton and the
Frozen Fiasco**

**Thea Stilton and the
Venice Masquerade**

**Thea Stilton and the
Niagara Splash**

**Thea Stilton and the
Riddle of the Ruins**

**Thea Stilton and the
Phantom of the Orchestra**

**Thea Stilton and the
Black Forest Burglary**

**Thea Stilton and the
Race for the Gold**

Don't miss a single fabumouse adventure!

#1 Lost Treasure of the Emerald Eye

#2 The Curse of the Cheese Pyramid

#3 Cat and Mouse in a Haunted House

#4 I'm Too Fond of My Fur!

#5 Four Mice Deep in the Jungle

#6 Paws Off, Cheddarface!

#7 Red Pizzas for a Blue Count

#8 Attack of the Bandit Cats

#9 A Fabumouse Vacation for Geronimo

#10 All Because of a Cup of Coffee

#11 It's Halloween, You 'Fraidy Mouse!

#12 Merry Christmas, Geronimo!

#13 The Phantom of the Subway

#14 The Temple of the Ruby of Fire

#15 The Mona Mousa Code

#16 A Cheese-Colored Camper

#17 Watch Your Whiskers, Stilton!

#18 Shipwreck on the Pirate Islands

#19 My Name Is Stilton, Geronimo Stilton

#20 Surf's Up, Geronimo!

#21 The Wild, Wild West

#22 The Secret of Cacklefur Castle

A Christmas Tale

#23 Valentine's Day Disaster

#24 Field Trip to Niagara Falls

#25 The Search for Sunken Treasure

#26 The Mummy with No Name

#27 The Christmas Toy Factory

#28 Wedding Crasher

#29 Down and Out Down Under

#30 The Mouse Island Marathon

#31 The Mysterious Cheese Thief

Christmas Catastrophe

#32 Valley of the Giant Skeletons

#33 Geronimo and the Gold Medal Mystery

#34 Geronimo Stilton, Secret Agent

#35 A Very Merry Christmas

#36 Geronimo's Valentine

#37 The Race Across America

#38 A Fabumouse School Adventure

#39 Singing Sensation

#40 The Karate Mouse

#41 Mighty Mount Kilimanjaro

#42 The Peculiar Pumpkin Thief

#43 I'm Not a Supermouse!

#44 The Giant Diamond Robbery

#45 Save the White Whale!

#46 The Haunted Castle

#47 Run for the Hills, Geronimo!

#48 The Mystery in Venice

#49 The Way of the Samurai

#50 This Hotel Is Haunted!

#51 The Enormouse Pearl Heist

#52 Mouse in Space!

#53 Rumble in the Jungle

#54 Get into Gear, Stilton!

#55 The Golden Statue Plot

#56 Flight of the Red Bandit

#57 The Stinky Cheese Vacation

#58 The Super Chef Contest

#59 Welcome to Moldy Manor

#60 The Treasure of Easter Island

#61 Mouse House Hunter

#62 Mouse Overboard!

#63 The Cheese Experiment

#64 Magical Mission

#65 Bollywood Burglary

#66 Operation: Secret Recipe

#67 The Chocolate Chase

#68 Cyber-Thief Showdown

#69 Hug a Tree, Geronimo

#70 The Phantom Bandit

#71 Geronimo on Ice!

#72 The Hawaiian Heist

#73 The Missing Movie

Up Next:

Don't miss any of my adventures in the Kingdom of Fantasy!

THE KINGDOM OF FANTASY

THE QUEST FOR PARADISE:
THE RETURN TO THE KINGDOM OF FANTASY

THE AMAZING VOYAGE:
THE THIRD ADVENTURE IN THE KINGDOM OF FANTASY

THE DRAGON PROPHECY:
THE FOURTH ADVENTURE IN THE KINGDOM OF FANTASY

THE VOLCANO OF FIRE:
THE FIFTH ADVENTURE IN THE KINGDOM OF FANTASY

THE SEARCH FOR TREASURE:
THE SIXTH ADVENTURE IN THE KINGDOM OF FANTASY

THE ENCHANTED CHARMS:
THE SEVENTH ADVENTURE IN THE KINGDOM OF FANTASY

THE PHOENIX OF DESTINY:
AN EPIC KINGDOM OF FANTASY ADVENTURE

THE HOUR OF MAGIC:
THE EIGHTH ADVENTURE IN THE KINGDOM OF FANTASY

THE WIZARD'S WAND:
THE NINTH ADVENTURE IN THE KINGDOM OF FANTASY

THE SHIP OF SECRETS:
THE TENTH ADVENTURE IN THE KINGDOM OF FANTASY

THE DRAGON OF FORTUNE:
AN EPIC KINGDOM OF FANTASY ADVENTURE

THE GUARDIAN OF THE REALM:
THE ELEVENTH ADVENTURE IN THE KINGDOM OF FANTASY

THE ISLAND OF DRAGONS:
THE TWELFTH ADVENTURE IN THE KINGDOM OF FANTASY